I Know My Name is Love

By Margaret Cate

Illustrated by: Rachael Mahaffey

ISBN: 1492117552
ISBN-13: 9781492117551
Library of Congress Control Number: 2013915157
CreateSpace Independent Publishing Platform
North Charleston, South Carolina

For my mother

Before the day of the thunderstorm, I always believed that my name was Mangy Mutt. I grew up on the streets as a puppy, begging for scraps of food and trying to survive. Most people just ignored me.

One day, a terrible storm came. Thunder and lightning filled the sky. I was afraid, and I hid under a tree. But the thunder startled me, so I ran out into the street, only inches from a car. The car's brakes squeaked and squealed as it came to a stop.

The car's windshield wipers went splish-splash-splosh against the glass. A gray-haired woman stepped out of the car. Her heels went clip-clap-clop against the pavement as she walked toward me. She said her name was Florence, and she asked me if I'd like to come and live with her. I leapt into her arms to be sure she knew I meant yes. She laughed and called me the best gift anyone could ever receive. She said she would name me Tilly.

~ 6 ~

Florence took me home and fed me the most delicious meal I had ever eaten. She even gave me a few table scraps. When I barked for more, she laughed and called me

Hope.

After dinner, Florence sat quietly reading a book. I rested my head on her knee to show her I was grateful that she had rescued me from the streets. She smiled and called me

Love.

~ 10 ~

The next day, Florence spent the morning bathing and grooming me in an avalanche of soap and shampoo. When she had finished, I felt like a different dog. I was no longer a mangy mutt. Florence called me

Beautiful.

I spent the afternoon chasing
squirrels around the backyard
and investigating inchworms.
Florence laughed and called me

Joy.

Then Florence took me for a walk in the park. I saw a little boy sitting by himself in a wheelchair. He looked sad as he watched the other children play. I ran to him and put my paws on his lap. A smile began to spread across his face. Then he giggled as I tried to lick his ear. The boy's mother called me

Miracle.

When Florence saw how happy I made the boy, she said, "I know just what to do." We drove home, and Florence began to train me for something very important.

My manners were a little rusty from living on the streets, but Florence helped me improve them. And one day, my training was complete. Florence dressed me in a vest printed with the word "Volunteer." We climbed into her car and drove to the children's hospital. I was very excited, because children are my favorite kind of humans.

~ 18 ~

Florence and I visited many people that day. There was Dr. Hayward, a surgeon, who needs glasses because she has sewn so many careful stitches over the years. I called her

Hope.

There was Nurse Nan, who has arthritis in her fingers from holding so many little hands.
I called her

Love.

~ 23 ~

There was Hannah in Room 403. She used to be sick and doesn't have any hair because of the medicine she took that has cured her. I called her

Beautiful.

There was Hector, who had broken his leg playing soccer. He has a big purple cast on his leg with a smiley face drawn on it. I called him

Joy.

Finally, there was Baby Benjamin in the nursery. He is the tiniest baby in the entire hospital, because he was born two months early. I called him *Miracle.*

I never knew my real name before I went to live with Florence that rainy day. No one called me anything but Mangy Mutt. Now I've learned that my name is Tilly, but it is also Hope, Love, Beautiful, Joy, and Miracle.

Love

Miracle

Hope

Beautiful

JOY

~ 30 ~

Whether you go by the name Dr. Hayward, Nurse Nan, Hannah, Hector, Baby Benjamin, or something else entirely, you too are known as Hope, Love, Beautiful, Joy, and Miracle. And you are the best gift anyone could ever receive.

Learn About
COLORS

Get ready to have some fun learning about colors with Elmo as you explore all the colors of the rainbow!

LEARN TO:

◆ Identify and match colors

◆ Read and write color words

◆ Recognize and continue color patterns

blue

orange

red

green

Family Activities

Name That Color
Sit down with your child and her favorite box of crayons. Take turns pulling crayons out of the box one at a time. Have her name the color of each crayon selected.

Color Clues
Give your child clues about an object that is a certain color and have him try to guess what the object is. For example: "This is something white. It looks fluffy. You see it high in the sky" (answer: a cloud). Now let your child give clues!

Colorful Days
Have your child pick a color of the day. For example, Monday is red day. Have fun wearing clothes, eating foods, and playing with toys that are that color all day!

Mix It Up
Use finger paints, water colors, or crayons to let your child experiment with mixing new colors. You might use these color combinations: yellow + blue = green, yellow + red = orange, blue + red = purple, white + red = pink, black + white = gray, green + red = brown.

Sock It To Me
Create color patterns using your child's socks. For example, put the following socks in a row: blue sock, white sock, blue sock, white sock. Together, discuss the color pattern and have her continue it by adding the sock color that comes next in the pattern.

Color Collage
Ask your child his favorite color. Then help him find and cut out pictures from old magazines, catalogs, and newspapers that show that color. Glue the pictures to a piece of construction paper to make a color collage.

Color Wheel
Help your child make a color wheel by dividing a paper plate into eight equal sections. Have her color each section a different color. Then take turns tossing a coin onto the color wheel. When the coin lands on a color, the player must name the color and identify an object that is the same color.

Book Walk
Go on a book walk with your child through his favorite picture book. Flip through the book page-by-page and look at the pictures together. Talk about all of the different colors the illustrator used and call attention to any unusual colors you see on your book walk.

4

Colorful Choo-Choo Trains

 Say the color of each train car.

 Then draw lines to match the train cars that are the same color.

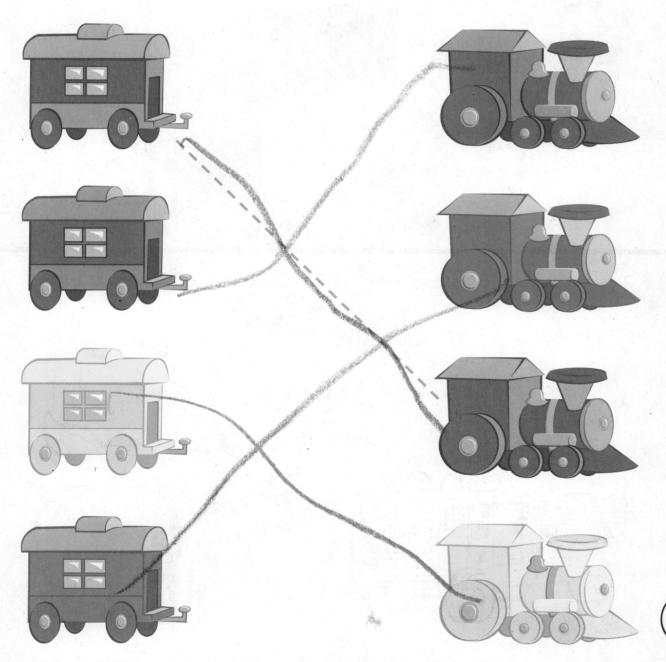

Ready, Set, Preschool! Learn About Colors

Learn About Red

Elmo likes his **red** monster truck the best.

 Circle the monster trucks that are **red**.

 Color the pictures **red**.

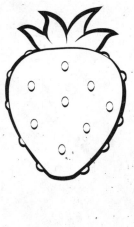

Learn About Blue

Cookie Monster wants to put his blueberries in **blue** bowls.

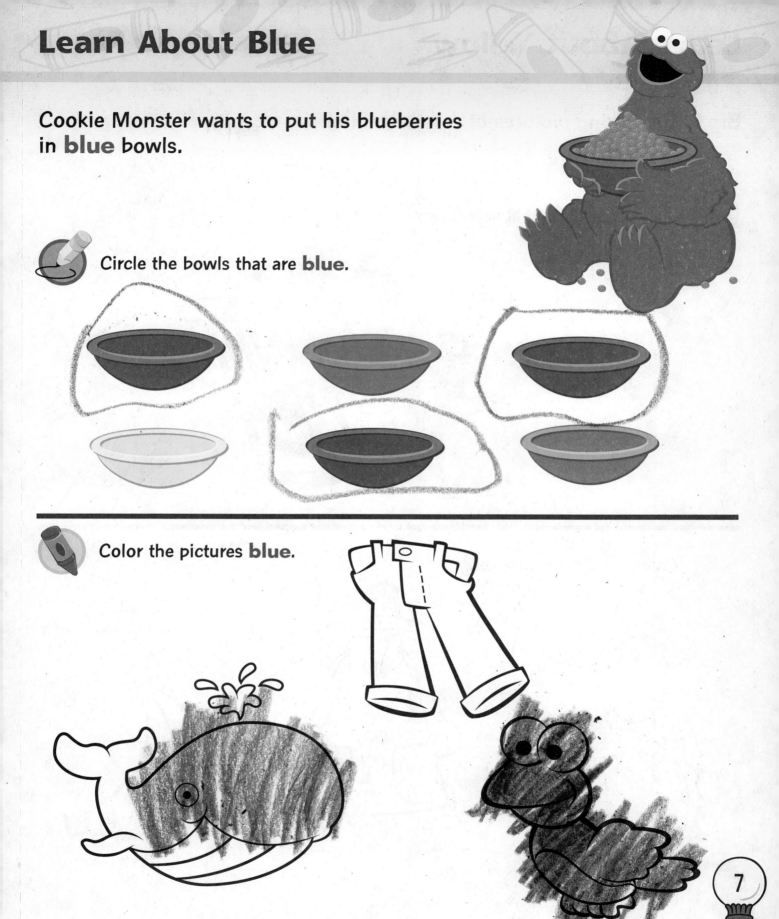

Circle the bowls that are **blue**.

Color the pictures **blue**.

SESAME STREET

Learn About Yellow

Big Bird is taking pictures of yellow things.

 Circle everything that is yellow.

 Color the pictures yellow.

8

Learn About Green

Oscar likes umbrellas that are **green** just like him.

 Draw an **X** on the umbrellas that are **green**.

 Color the pictures **green**.

Ready, Set, Preschool! Learn About Colors   SESAME STREET

Learn About Purple

Elmo is helping Two-Headed Monster pick out **purple** foods.

 Circle the foods that are **purple**.

Color the pictures **purple**.

10

Learn About Orange

Zoe is looking for orange fish.

 Circle the fish that are orange.

 Color the pictures orange.

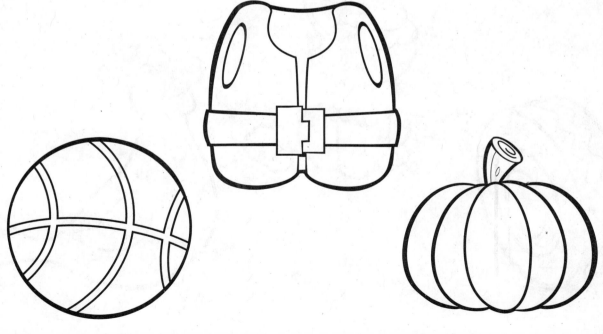

Learn About Black

The Count wears **black** capes.

 Circle the **black** capes.

 Color the pictures **black**.

Learn About Brown

Baby Bear needs a **brown** crayon to finish his picture.

 Circle the crayons that are **brown.**

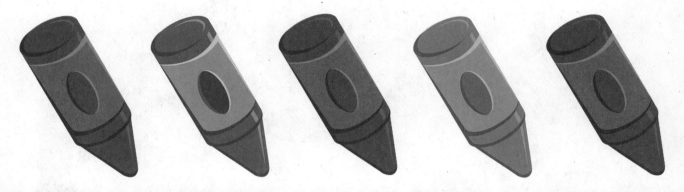

 Color the pictures **brown.**

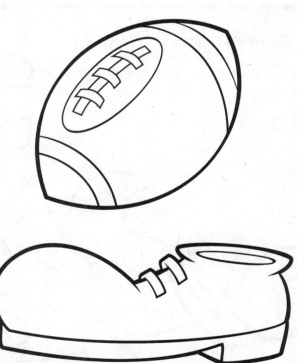

13

Learn About Gray

Oscar likes things that are **gray** like his garbage can.

 Draw an **X** on everything that is **gray**.

 Color the pictures **gray**.

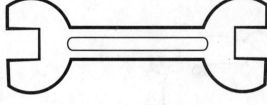

 14

Learn About Pink

Telly and Elmo are drawing with pink chalk.

 Circle the pink chalk drawings.

Color the pictures pink.

15

Learn About White

The Amazing Mumford is pulling a white rabbit out of a hat.

 Circle all the rabbits that are white.

  Think of three things that are white.
Then draw one of them.

16

Elmo the Painter

Elmo needs your help to finish his painting.

 Color the spaces the same color as the dots.

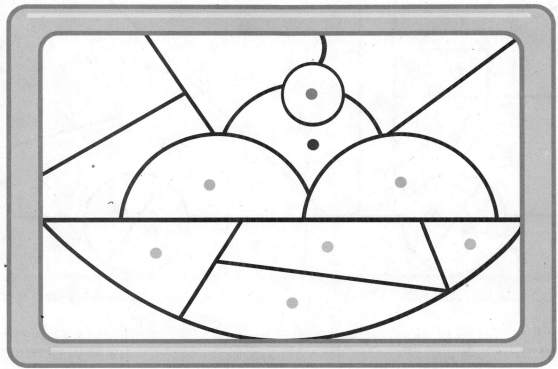

What did you make?

_____

 Color each can of paint to match the color word.

red   orange   pink   brown

17

A Surprise Picture

 Color the spaces the same color as the dots.

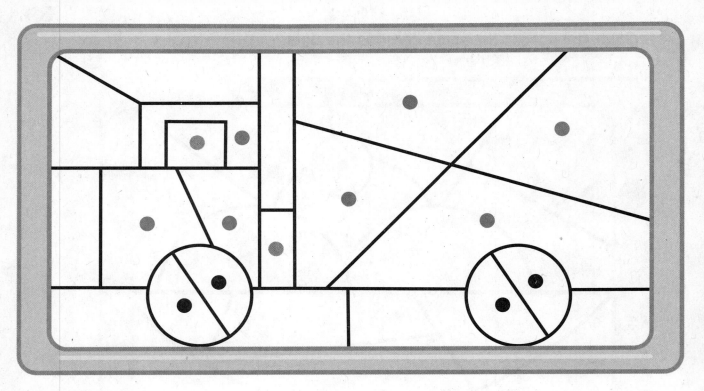

What did you make?

 Color each can of paint to match the color word.

blue   purple   black   gray

 Explore More ■ ◆ ● ■ ● ◆ ■ ● ◆ ■ ●

The next time you are at the grocery store, encourage your child to identify the different colors of fruits, vegetables, and other foods. You can help your child make a color list to bring to the store. Then prompt him or her to look for all the colors on the list.

18

Another Colorful Painting

Elmo needs your help again.

 Color the spaces the same color as the dots.

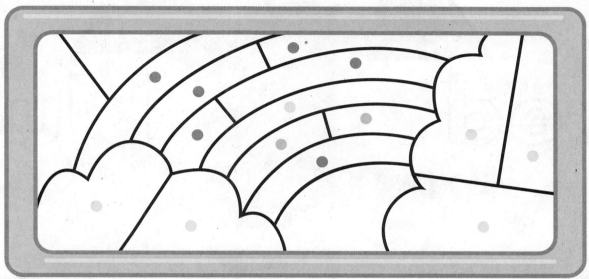

What did you make?

 Color each can of paint to match the color word.

green

blue

red

yellow

purple

orange

Red Triangle, Blue Triangle

Telly collects triangles. He has a **red** triangle and a **blue** triangle.

Color the words **red** and **blue**.

red   blue

 Trace the color word **red**.

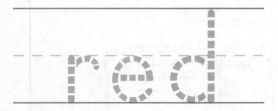

 Color the triangle to match.

 Trace the color word **blue**.

 Color the triangle to match.

20

Little Tugboats

Color the tugboats.

 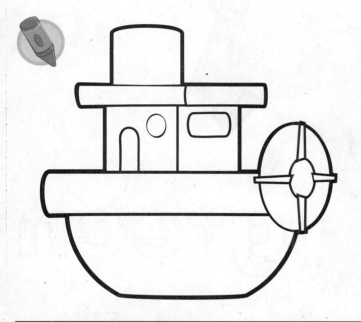

 Make your own picture using **red** and **blue**.

SESAME STREET

Yellow Tie, Green Tie

Color the words and **green**.

yellow

green

 Trace the color word *yellow*.

yellow

 Color the tie to match.

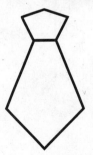

 Trace the color word **green**.

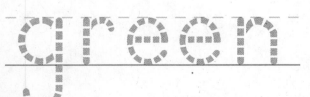

green

 Color the tie to match.

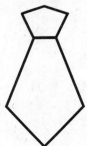

22

Buggy Bugs

Color the bugs.

  Make your own picture using **yellow** and **green**.

23

Purple Juice, Orange Juice

Zoe likes juice. She drinks **purple** juice and **orange** juice.

Color the words **purple** and **orange**.

 Trace the color word **purple**.

 Color the juice to match.

 Trace the color word **orange**.

 Color the juice to match.

Colorful Kites

Color the kites.

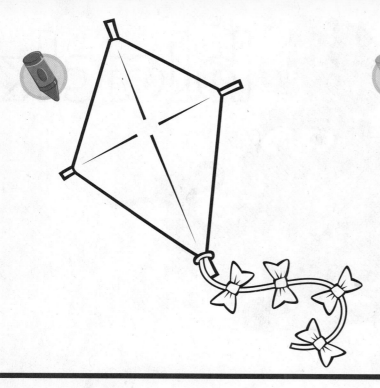

  Make your own picture using **purple** and orange.

Black Hat, Brown Shoes

Snuffy loves to dance. He's wearing a **black** hat and **brown** shoes.

Color the words **black** and **brown**.

black

brown

 Trace the color word **black**.

black

 Color the hat to match.

 Trace the color word **brown**.

brown

 Color the shoe to match.

Cute Little Puppies

Color the puppies.

  Make your own picture using **black** and **brown**.

27

123 SESAME STREET

Gray Helmet, Pink Cape

Look! It's Super Grover! He has a **gray** helmet and a **pink** cape.

Color the words **gray** and **pink**.

gray

pink

 Trace the color word **gray**.

gray

 Color the helmet to match.

 Trace the color word **pink**.

pink

 Color the cape to match.

Elephants on Parade

Color the elephants.

  Make your own picture using **gray** and **pink**.

29

White Cake

Ernie loves cake. He has a white cake.

Color the word white.

 Trace the color word white.

Color the cake to match.

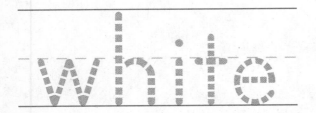

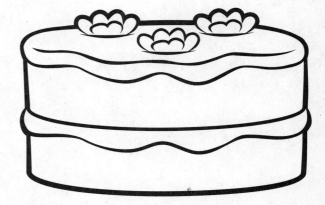

Socks by the Pair

Help Elmo match his socks.

 Draw lines to match the socks that are the same color.

SESAME STREET

Tea for Two

Cookie Monster and Prairie Dawn are having a tea party.

 Draw lines to match the teacups that are the same color.

SESAME STREET Ready, Set, Preschool! Learn About Colors

Pairs for Hair

Elmo is helping Zoe look for a pair of hair bows that match.

 Draw lines to match the hair bows that are the same color.

A Feather in Your Hat

Elmo and Grover like to dress up as pirates.

 Draw lines to match the feathers and hats that are the same color.

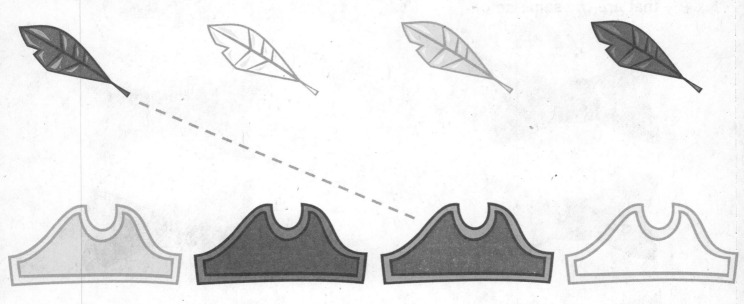

 Color this feather and hat any colors you want.

 34

Platefuls of Colors

Help Elmo and Telly put these fruits where they belong.

 Draw lines to match the fruits and plates that are the same color.

  Draw your favorite fruit. Then color it.

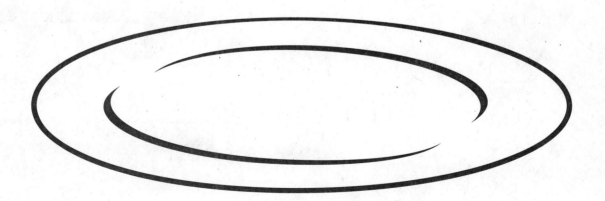

Ready, Set, Preschool! Learn About Colors

SESAME STREET

At the Library

Elmo and Big Bird need to sort the books by color.

 Draw lines to match each book to the shelf that is the same color.

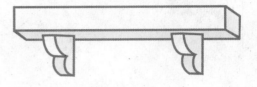

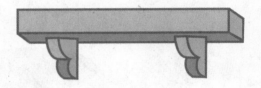

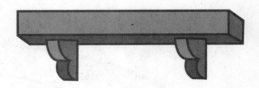

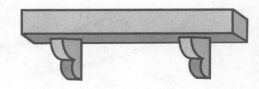

Clean-up Time

Bert and Ernie need to pick up the toys.

 Draw lines to match each toy with the box that is the same color.

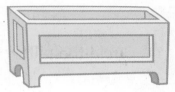

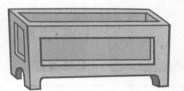

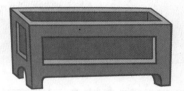

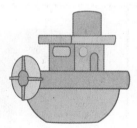

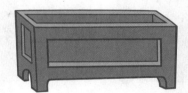

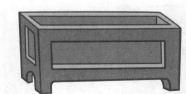

Explore More

Clean-up time can be a great time to practice grouping things by color. Help your child label storage containers by color. Then encourage him or her to sort toys by color by putting them in the containers with the matching color word. Try this with laundry, too.

Ready, Set, Preschool! Learn About Colors

Pillow Patterns

Elmo is helping The Count make
a pattern with pillows.

 Circle the pillow that comes next in each pattern.

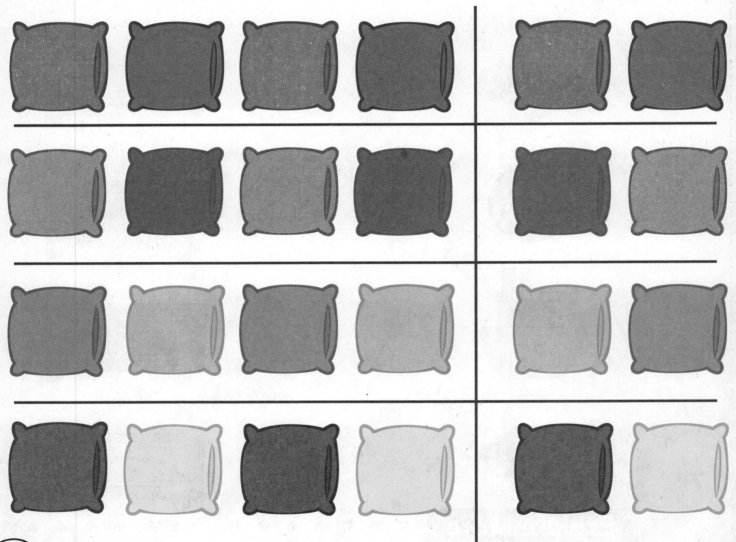

Put Your Heart into Patterns

Rosita is making a pattern with hearts.

 Circle the heart that comes next in each pattern.

Ready, Set, Preschool! Learn About Colors   SESAME STREET

Pretty Flowers in a Row

Elmo is helping Prairie Dawn plant flowers in pretty patterns.

 Circle the flower that comes next in each pattern.

Ready, Set, Preschool! Learn About Colors

Continue the Patterns

Elmo likes different shapes and colors.

 Color the shape to continue each pattern.

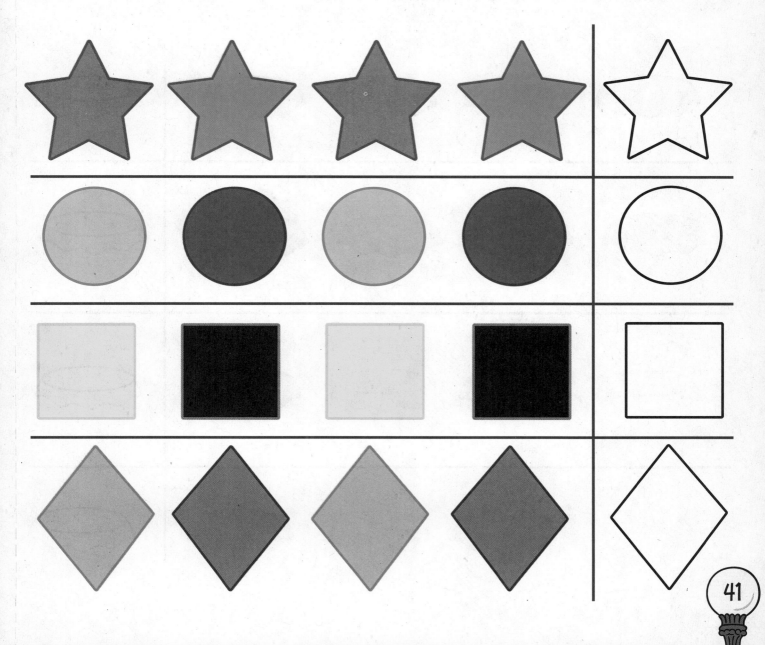

SESAME STREET

Bert's Bottle Caps

Bert is making a pattern with his bottle caps.

 Color the bottle cap to continue each pattern.

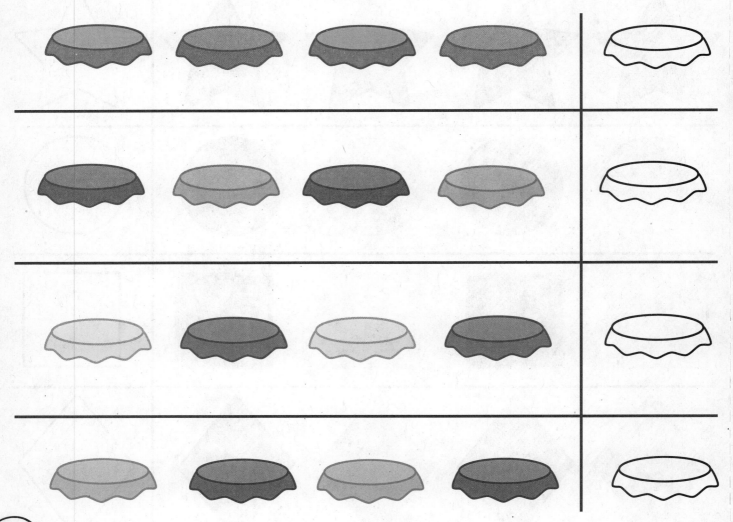

Ready, Set, Preschool! Learn About Colors

Zoe's Necklace

Elmo is helping Zoe make a necklace.

 Color the bead to continue each pattern.

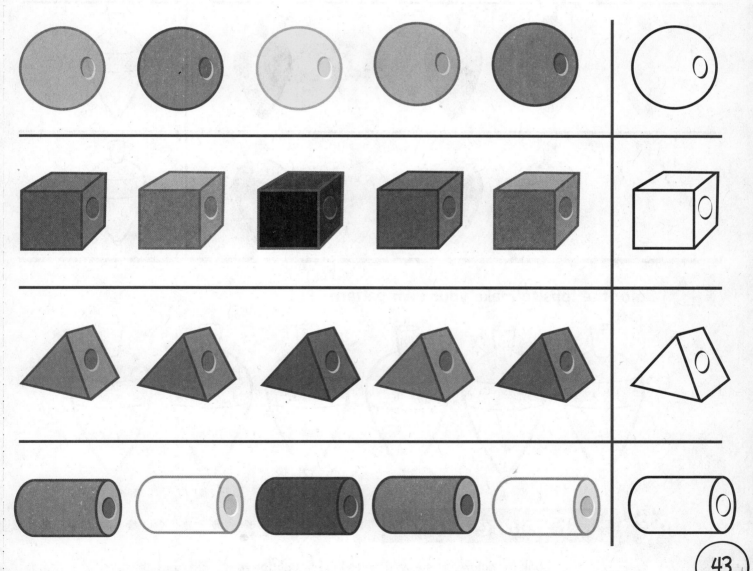

Ready, Set, Preschool! Learn About Colors

SESAME STREET

Elmo's Toy Tops

Elmo is playing with toy tops.

 Color the toy top to continue each pattern.

 Color the tops to make your own pattern.

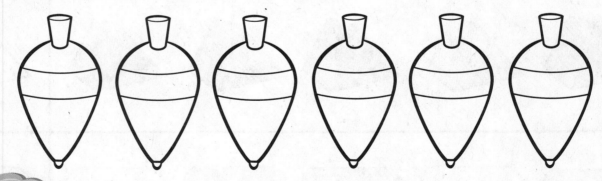

 Explore More

Look for colored pasta with holes big enough for your child to easily put onto a string. Encourage your child to make color patterns using the uncooked pasta. Then help him or her make a colorful necklace.

Green Monster Punch

Yellow and blue make **green**.

Circle the **green** punch.

Now that Oscar has his punch, he wants to have a **green** monster party.

Color everything **green** for the party.

45

Squishy Orange Clay

Yellow and red make orange.

 Circle the orange clay.

Now that Ernie has his clay, he wants to make some orange things.

Color everything orange.

SESAME STREET   Ready, Set, Preschool! Learn About Colors

Yummy Purple Cupcakes

Blue and red make **purple**.

Circle the **purple** icing.

Now that Two-Headed Monster has **purple** icing, he wants to frost his cupcakes.

Color all the cupcakes **purple**.

47

SESAME STREET

Pink Strawberry Milk

White and red make pink.

 Circle the pink milk.

Now that Telly has his pink strawberry milk, he wants to share it with his friends.

 Color the glasses of milk pink.

Gray Paint

Black and white make **gray**.

Circle the **gray** paint.

Now that The Count has **gray** paint, he wants to paint a castle wall.

Color the wall **gray**.

49

Brown Bear

Green and red make **brown**.

 Circle the **brown** paint.

Now that Baby Bear has **brown** paint, he wants to paint a picture.

 Color the picture **brown**.

50

Colors to Wear

 Color the paint bottles that are used to make each color.

Big Bird wants an orange shirt.

Zoe wants a purple shirt.

Oscar wants a brown shirt.

My Favorite Color

Elmo wants to know what color is your favorite!

 Draw a picture and color it with your favorite colors.

Explore More

Play "I Spy My Favorite Color" with your child. Find something in the room that you and your child are in, that is your favorite color. Give your child clues about the object until he or she guesses what it is. Then switch roles with your child and play again.

52

 Ready, Set, Preschool! Learn About Colors

Learn About LETTERS

Set off on an alphabet adventure with Cookie Monster as you explore all the letters of the alphabet!

LEARN TO:
- Identify letters (uppercase and lowercase)
- Recognize letter sounds
- Trace and write letters

Family Activities

Name Game
Have your child say the name of each member of your family. Talk about the sound at the beginning of each name. Then, help him write the uppercase letter that stands for each beginning sound.

Crafty Letters
Gather some craft supplies that can be used creatively to make different upper and lowercase letters. For example, your child can make letters using yarn, toothpicks, glitter, glue, buttons, or pipe cleaners.

Tall or Small?
Help your child write five uppercase and five lowercase letters on separate index cards. Mix up the cards and show them to her one at a time. Have her stand up tall if you display an uppercase letter, and crouch down small if you display a lowercase letter.

Guess The Letter
Use your index finger to "draw" an uppercase letter on your child's back. Have him guess which letter you drew. Then switch, and let him draw a letter on your back and you guess the letter.

Partner Up
At the top of a large sheet of paper, write one uppercase or lowercase letter. Next to the letter you write, ask your child to write the matching letter partner. For example, if you write uppercase **T**, she should write lowercase **t**, or if you write lowercase **b**, she should write uppercase **B**. Repeat the activity for different letters of the alphabet.

What's Cooking?
Food labels are full of letters to learn. Together with your child, look at labels on food containers. Ask him to name the letters that he recognizes. You may also ask him to find a specific letter, such as uppercase **P** or lowercase **c**.

Silly Sentences
Make up silly sentences that contain several words that begin with the same sound. Say each sentence and ask your child to identify the letter sound that is repeated. For example, Messy Max makes meatball milkshakes (**m**). Now have her pick a letter and make up a silly sentence for you to guess the letter sound.

Grab Bag
Help your child write all of the lowercase letters of the alphabet on individual slips of paper. Put all of the slips into a paper bag. Have him reach in and pull out one slip at a time. Have him name the letter on the slip and tell what sound the letter makes. To extend the activity, have him name a word that begins with that letter sound.

54

Beginning with Big Letters

Letters come in big and small sizes! The big form of each letter
is called **uppercase**. Cookie Monster's cookie has an uppercase **C**.

 Color each cookie that has an uppercase letter on it.

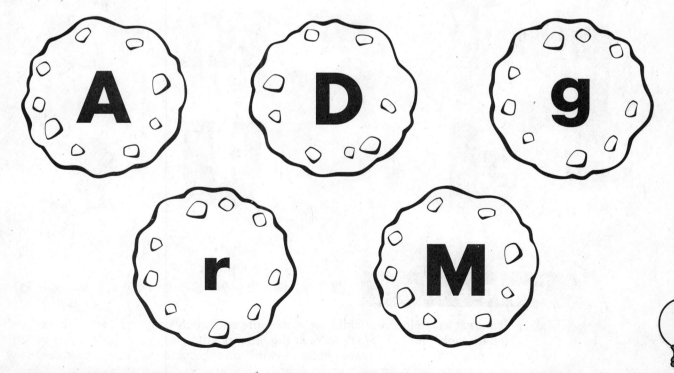

55

Searching for Small Letters

The small form of each letter is called **lowercase**.
Cookie Monster's cookie has a lowercase **c**.

 Circle the lowercase letters.

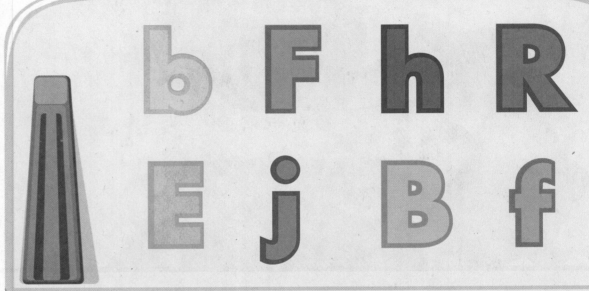

b F h R

E j B f

T e m G

d N U t

Explore More ■ ◆ ● ■ ◆ ● ■ ◆ ●

It's great to remind your child about the differences between how uppercase and lowercase letters look. The next time you're at the grocery store with your child, point out the use of uppercase and lowercase letters in words on signs and items on the shelves.

 Ready, Set, Preschool! Learn About Letters

Awesome A

A and **a** are letter partners.

  Trace each **A** and **a**. Then write some of your own.

 Color each picture whose name begins with **a**.

apple   **Bert**   **ant**

57

Bouncing with B

   B **b**

B and **b** are letter partners.

 Trace each **B** and **b**. Then write some of your own.

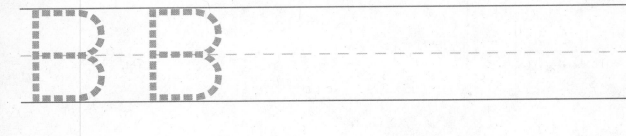

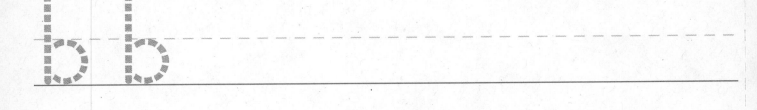

 Circle each picture whose name begins with **b**.

fan   **bat**   **ball**

58

C Is for Cookie

C and c are letter partners.

  Trace each **C** and **c**. Then write some of your own.

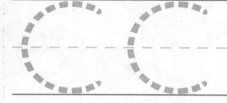

 Color each picture whose name begins with **c**.

sun   **carrot**   **cake**

Following A, B, and C

Help Cookie Monster get to Sesame Street.

Draw a line through the path that shows cookies with the letters **A**, **B**, and **C**.

Dandy Letter D

D and **d** are letter partners.

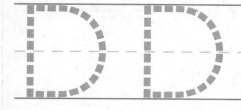 Trace each **D** and **d**. Then write some of your own.

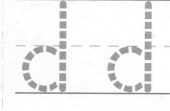

 Circle each picture whose name begins with **d**.

door　　　　　　**tree**　　　　　　**drum**

Ready, Set, Preschool! Learn About Letters

Excellent E

E and **e** are letter partners.

 Trace each **E** and **e**. Then write some of your own.

E E

e e

 Color each picture whose name begins with **e**.

  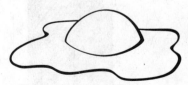

envelope   **dog**   **egg**

Fishing for F

F and **f** are letter partners.

 Trace each **F** and **f**. Then write some of your own.

F F

f f

 Circle each picture whose name begins with **f**.

fish

book

five

Ready, Set, Preschool! Learn About Letters

SESAME STREET

Clean-up Time

Help Cookie Monster put away his blocks.

 Draw a line from each box to the block that shows its letter partner.

SESAME STREET Ready, Set, Preschool! Learn About Letters

Out to Sea

  Say the name of each letter you see. Color the spaces using the color key.

Color Key

A=   B=   C=   D=   E=   F=

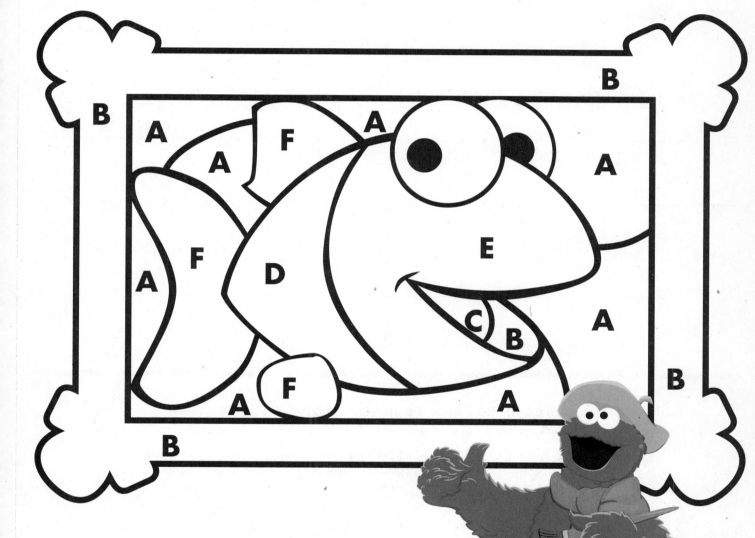

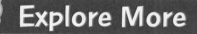

Encourage your child to have fun practicing letters! Sprinkle sand, sugar, or powdered drink mix on a cookie sheet. Have your child use his or her index finger to practice writing **A, B, C, D, E,** and **F.**

65

 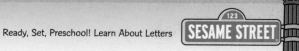

G Is Great

  G g

G and **g** are letter partners.

 Trace each **G** and **g**. Then write some of your own.

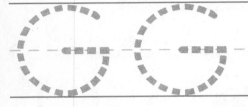 G G G

g g

 Color each picture whose name begins with **g**.

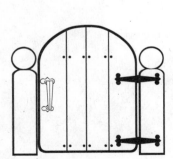  

gate   **bottle**   **grapes**

 66

SESAME STREET   Ready, Set, Preschool! Learn About Letters

Hats off for H

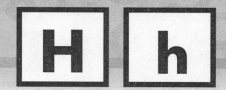

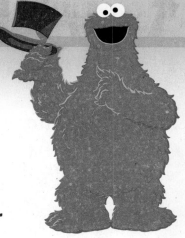

H and **h** are letter partners.

 Trace each **H** and **h**. Then write some of your own.

H H H

h h h

 Circle each picture whose name begins with **h**.

kitten   **hammer**   **hat**

Ready, Set, Preschool! Learn About Letters

 SESAME STREET

Incredible I

I and **i** are letter partners.

  Trace each **I** and **i**. Then write some of your own.

I I

i i

 Color each picture whose name begins with **i**.

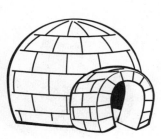  

igloo   **cow**   **ink**

Gg-Hh-Ii Hunt

Help Cookie Monster find the hidden letters.

Find and circle **G**, **H**, and **I**.
Then find and circle **g**, **h**, and **i**.

69

SESAME STREET

Jumping for J

J and **j** are letter partners.

 Trace each **J** and **j**. Then write some of your own.

J   J

j   j

 Circle each picture whose name begins with **j**.

duck

jacket

jar

Keeping up with K

K and **k** are letter partners.

  Trace each **K** and **k**. Then write some of your own.

K K

k k

 Color each picture whose name begins with **k**.

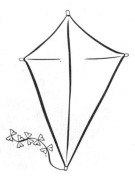

kite   **key**   **bee**

71

Look out for L

L and I are letter partners.

  Trace each **L** and **I**. Then write some of your own.

 Circle each picture whose name begins with **I**.

lamp

lion

frog

 Ready, Set, Preschool! Learn About Letters

M and **m** are letter partners.

  Trace each **M** and **m**. Then write some of your own.

 Color each picture whose name begins with **m**.

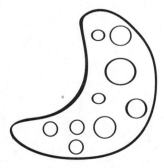

moon   **mitten**   **leaf**

73

Color by Letter

Cookie Monster wants to color these pictures.
You can help him!

  Say the names of the letter partners on each picture.
Then color the pictures using the color key.

Color Key

Jj =    Kk =   Ll =    Mm =

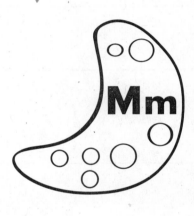

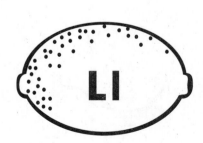

Monster Match–up

Help Cookie Monster match the cookies.

 Draw lines to match the cookies with their letter partners.

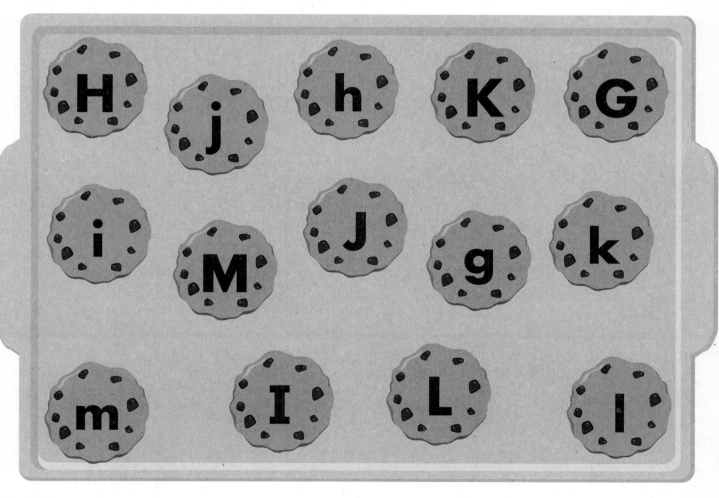

H   j   h   K   G

i   M   J   g   k

m   I   L   l

Explore More ■ ◆ ● ■ ◆ ● ■ ◆ ● ■ ◆ ●

Turn learning about letters into a game! Play tic-tac-toe with your child. Instead of using **X** and **O**, use letter partners like **G** and **g** or **M** and **m**.

75

N Is Very Nice

 **N** **n**

N and **n** are letter partners.

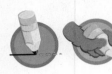 Trace each **N** and **n**. Then write some of your own.

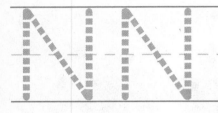

 Circle each picture whose name begins with **n**.

nail   **mouse**   **nine**

O Is Out of This World

O and **o** are letter partners.

  Trace each **O** and **o**. Then write some of your own.

 Color each picture whose name begins with **o**.

octopus　　　**Grover**　　　**owl**

 77

Perfectly P

P and p are letter partners.

  Trace each **P** and **p**. Then write some of your own.

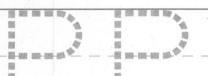

 Circle each picture whose name begins with **p**.

tire   **pear**   **pie**

 Ready, Set, Preschool! Learn About Letters

Now On to Presents!

Help Cookie Monster match the presents.

 Draw lines from each big present to the little presents that show its letter partner.

P   N   O

o   n   p   o   n

 **Explore More** ◆ ■ ● ◆ ■ ● ◆ ■ ● ◆ ■

Go through old newspapers with your child. Encourage him or her to find examples of letter partners such as **P** and **p**. Cut out the letters and glue them onto a sheet of paper to make a letter collage.

Quiet Q

Q and q are letter partners.

  Trace each **Q** and **q**. Then write some of your own.

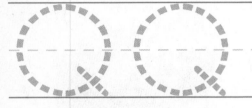

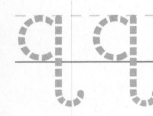

 Color each picture whose name begins with **q**.

queen

Rosita

quilt

 Ready, Set, Preschool! Learn About Letters

Remarkable R

R and **r** are letter partners.

  Trace each **R** and **r**. Then write some of your own.

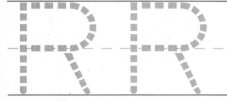

 Circle each picture whose name begins with **r**.

cup **robe** **rug**

81

Super S

S and s are letter partners.

 Trace each **S** and **s**.
Then write some of your own.

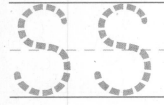

 Color each picture whose name begins with **s**.

82

snake **seal** **car**

Finding Qq, Rr, and Ss

Help Cookie Monster find the letters hidden in the picture.

Look for big letters first! Find and circle **Q**, **R**, and **S**. Then find and circle **q**, **r**, and **s**.

Explore More ◆ ■ ● ■ ◆ ● ◆ ■ ● ■ ◆ ■

Help your child form letters with cold cooked spaghetti noodles. If you form the letters on wax paper, you can let them dry and harden. Then you can glue them on paper and paint or color them!

83

Terrific T

T and **t** are letter partners.

 Trace each **T** and **t**. Then write some of your own.

 Circle each picture whose name begins with **t**.

truck　　　　　　　　**plane**　　　　　　　　**turtle**

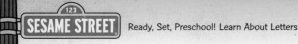

Unique U

U and **u** are letter partners.

 Trace each **U** and **u**. Then write some of your own.

U U

u u

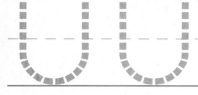 Color each picture whose name begins with **u**.

unicorn

pillow

umbrella

Valuable V

V and **v** are letter partners.

  Trace each **V** and **v**.
Then write some of your own.

 Circle each picture whose name begins with **v**.

Snuffy

van

vase

Move It!

Cookie Monster sees some moving vans.

 Color the wheel that has the letter partner on it.

87

Ready, Set, Preschool! Learn About Letters   SESAME STREET

Wonderful W

W w

W and w are letter partners.

  Trace each **W** and **w**.
Then write some of your own.

W W W

w w

 Color each picture whose name begins with **w**.

watch   **well**   **mop**

 Ready, Set, Preschool! Learn About Letters

X–tra Special X

X and **x** are letter partners.

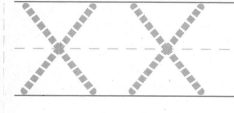 Trace each **X** and **x**. Then write some of your own.

 Circle each picture whose name begins with **x**.

xylophone

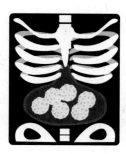

x-ray

fish

89

Yippee for Y

Y **y**

Y and y are letter partners.

  Trace each **Y** and **y**. Then write some of your own.

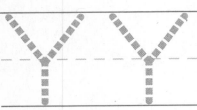

 Color each picture whose name begins with **y**.

  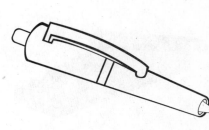

yogurt   **yak**   **pen**

90

Zany About Z

Z z

Z and z are letter partners.

  Trace each **Z** and **z**. Then write some of your own.

Circle each picture whose name begins with **z**.

zebra   **Elmo**   **zero**

91

A Picture for You

  Say the name of each letter you see.
Color the spaces using the color key.

Color Key

W =   **X =**   **Y =**   **Z =**

Ready, Set, Preschool! Learn About Letters

Noodle Partners

Uh—oh! Cookie Monster's alphabet soup spilled.

Draw lines to match the noodles that are letter partners.

Ready, Set, Preschool! Learn About Letters

SESAME STREET

A Big Letter Party

Come join the party!

 Color all of the balloons with uppercase letters.

Get Your Party Hat

Big Bird and Snuffy are wearing party hats.

 Color all of the party hats with uppercase letters.

 F  M  P  I

 a  S  n  G

 Write the uppercase letter that your name begins with on this party hat.

Ready, Set, Preschool! Learn About Letters

SESAME STREET

A Little Letter Party

Little letter presents.

 Draw an **X** on all of the presents with lowercase letters.

Time for Cake

Cookie Monster is ready for cake!

 Color all of the cakes with lowercase letters.

 b  L  Y  j

 Q  e  D w

 Trace the lowercase letters.

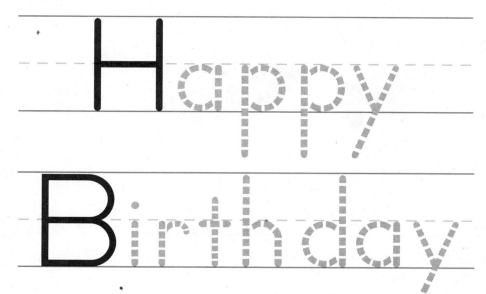

Happy
Birthday

Practice A to Z

Say the name of each picture. Then trace the letter.

a   b   c

j   k   l   m   n   o

v   w   x   y   z

d e f g h i

p q r s t u

Explore More

Help your child practice naming letters by playing a fun "Letter Alarm" game. Pretend you are sleeping and only "wake up" when your child shouts the letter you're "dreaming" about.

99

Ready, Set, Preschool! Learn About Letters   SESAME STREET

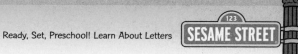

Super Letter Maze

Help Cookie Monster and Prairie Dawn go from **Aa** to **Zz**.

 Draw a line through the path that shows the correct letter partners.

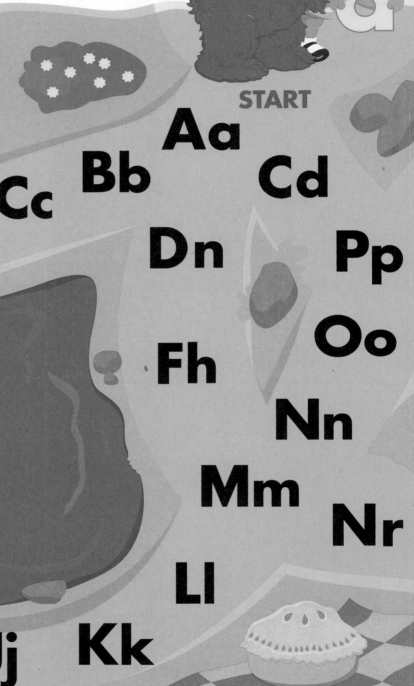

START

Aa
Bb   Cd
Cc
Dd   Dn   Pp
Ee
Ff   Fh   Oo
Nn
Gg   Mm   Nr
Hh   Ll
Ii   Jj   Kk

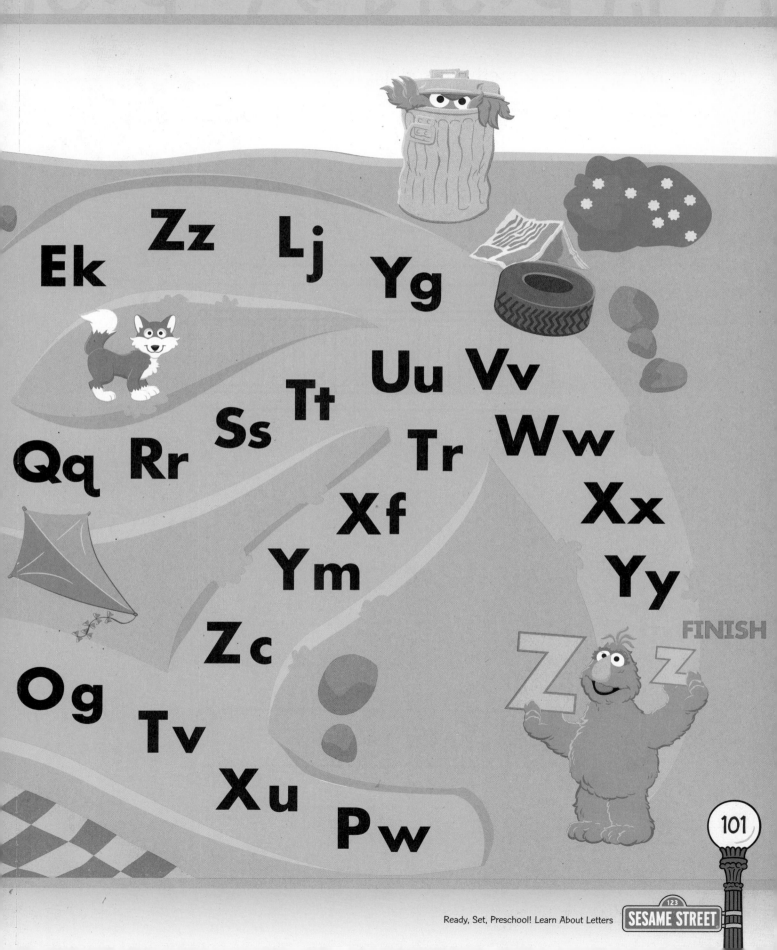

Ek Zz Lj Yg

Uu Vv

Ss Tt Tr Ww

Qq Rr Xf Xx

Ym Yy

Zc FINISH

Og Tv Zz Z

Xu Pw

101

Ready, Set, Preschool! Learn About Letters

SESAME STREET

Letter Champion

Cookie Monster has something special just for you!

Draw lines to connect the dots from **A** to **Z**.

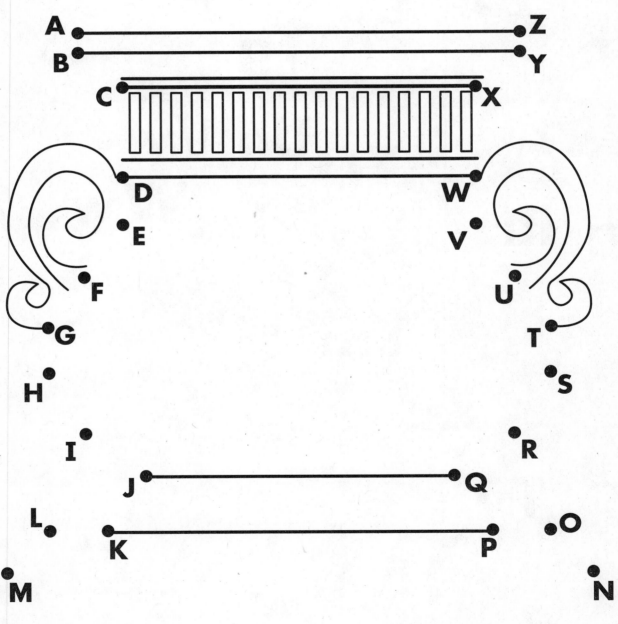

A ·   · Z
B ·   · Y
C ·   · X
D ·   · W
· E   · V
· F   U
· G   · T
· H   · S
· I   · R
J ·   · Q
L ·   · O
K ·   · P
· M   · N

SESAME STREET   Ready, Set, Preschool! Learn About Letters

Find the Letters

Cookie Monster loves looking for letters!

Look at the letters in the box. Then find and circle those letters in the picture.

O   M   C   Y   S

Ready, Set, Preschool! Learn About Letters

SESAME STREET

My Very Own Letters

You have learned a lot about letters!

Share what you know!

 Write your name on the line.

_____

- -

_____

 Draw a picture of something that begins with the same letter as your name. Color it.

Learn About COUNTING

Count bats and hats and trucks and ducks as you explore numbers from 1 to 20 with The Count!

LEARN TO:
- ◆ Count by 1's (to 20)
- ◆ Count down from 10 to 1
- ◆ Trace and write numbers
- ◆ Group numbers
- ◆ Add numbers up to 10

1 one

2 two

3 three

Family Activities

Counting In The Kitchen

The kitchen is a good place for your child to practice counting skills. Assemble things to count, such as pots and pans, or soup cans. Place 1-5 objects in front of her and have her count them. Then, increase the number of objects to 10, then to 15, and eventually to 20.

Numbers Here, There, and Everywhere

Take your child on a walk through your neighborhood. Look for numbers on houses, cars, street signs, stores, and other buildings. Have him identify the numbers he recognizes. Talk about how numbers help us in our daily lives.

How Old Are You?

Ask your child to tell how old she is. Help her write the number that shows her age on a sheet of paper. Then have her draw a birthday cake with the corresponding number of candles.

Ten Toys

Have your child pick ten favorite toys. Help him sort the toys into three or four groups. For example, he may sort the toys by size, color, or purpose. Ask him to count the toys in each group. Then have him count the total number of toys. As your child's skills build, increase the number of toys to twenty.

Helping Hands

Help your child trace both of her hands on a large sheet of paper. Count the fingers on one hand together and then ask her to count the fingers on both hands. Talk about all of the things your hands help you do.

Up and Down

Turn climbing the stairs into a learning game. Have your child count the stairs as you climb them together. Then help him count backwards as you to go down the stairs together.

Family Calendar

Make a family calendar for the current month on a large sheet of paper. Help your child label the squares on the calendar with the numbers 1-30 or 1-31. Talk about and label special family days on the calendar such as vacations, birthdays, or other occasions.

Important Numbers

Write your phone number and address on a sheet of paper. Talk with your child about the numbers, what they mean, and why they are important to know. Have her repeat each number after you and then have her practice saying them on her own.

Let's Count!

The Count loves to count!

  Count and color **3** bats.

Ready, Set, Preschool! Learn About Counting

SESAME STREET

The Number 1

The Count is ready to start counting.

  Count and color **1** castle.

  Trace the number **1**. Then write some of your own.

108

Count to 1

 Circle each group with **1**.

 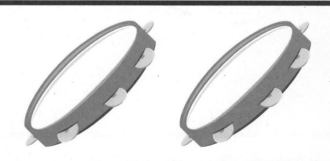

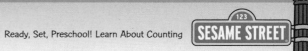

2 two

Zoe wears ballet slippers when she dances.

  Count and color **2** ballet slippers.

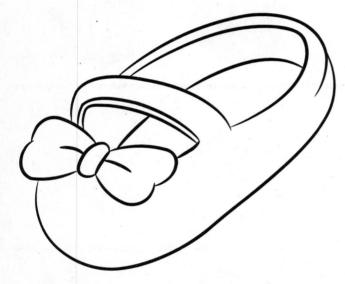 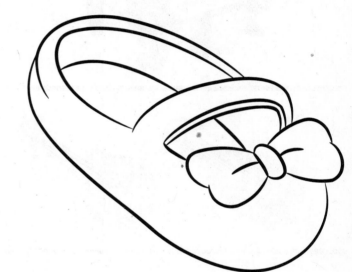

 Trace the number **2**. Then write some of your own.

2 2

Count to 2

 Circle each group with **2**.

Explore More

Help your child count the shoes in his closet. First count each pair of shoes.
Then count each shoe. Have fun counting other things that come in pairs, such
as socks or mittens.

The Number 3

Elmo is playing with monster trucks.

  Count and color **3** monster trucks.

  Trace the number **3**. Then write some of your own.

112

3 3

Count to 3

 Circle each group with **3**.

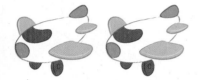  

Ready, Set, Preschool! Learn About Counting

SESAME STREET

The Number 4

Snuffy is having fun skating.

  Count and color **4** roller skates.

  Trace the number **4**. Then write some of your own.

114

  Draw **4** stripes on each rocket.
Then circle **4** rockets.

115

The Number 5

Big Bird is going fishing.

  Count and color **5** fish.

  Trace the number **5**. Then write some of your own.

116

Count to 5

 Circle **5** birds.
Then draw more boats to make **5** in all.

Explore More ■ ◆ ● ■ ◆ ● ◆ ● ■ ◆ ●

Give your child a "hand" at counting! Have your child practice counting from
1 to **5** by counting the fingers on one of your hands. Your child may have fun
counting toes too!

117

Grover in Space

Super Grover thinks counting is out of this world!

  Say the numbers in the picture.
Then color the spaces using the color key.

1=   2=   3=   4=   5=

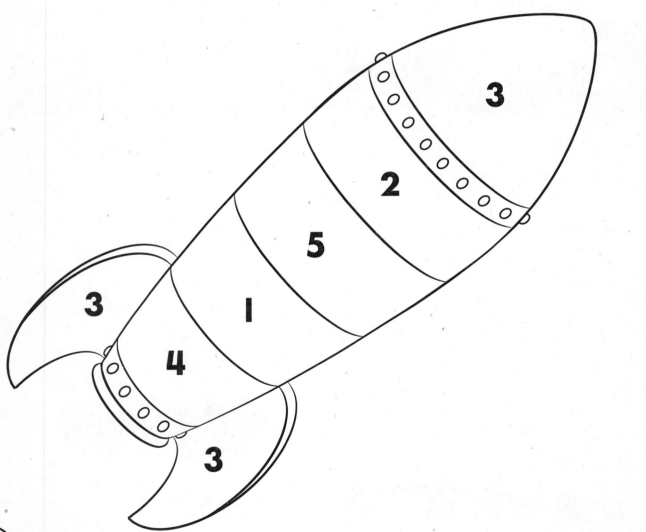

Count Your Lucky Stars

 Count the stars in each group.
Then circle the number that comes next.

1   **2**    **3**    **4**

3    **4**    **3**    **5**

2   **3**    **5**    **4**

3    **4**    **5**    **2**

119

The Number 6

Cookie Monster eats cookies while
The Count counts them.

  Count and color **6** cookies..

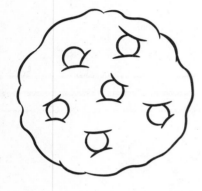 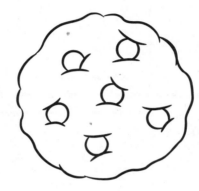 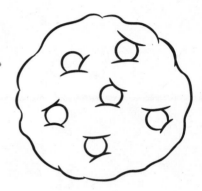

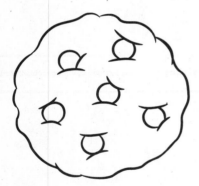 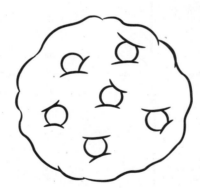 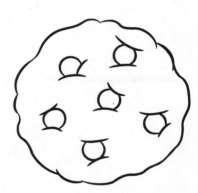

  Trace the number **6**. Then write some of your own.

Count to 6

The Count put some candles on the cakes.

  Color **6** cakes.
Then circle the cakes with **6** candles.

The Number 7

Ernie loves to take a bath.

  Count and color **7** rubber duckies.

  Trace the number **7.** Then write some of your own.

7 7

Ready, Set, Preschool! Learn About Counting

Count to 7

7

Draw lines from groups of **7** to the number.
Then color the groups of **7**.

7

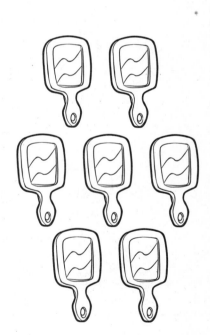

123

The Number 8

Bert and Bernice are visiting the pigeons in the park.

  Count and color **8** pigeons.

  Trace the number **8.** Then write some of your own.

124

Count to 8

Circle **8** birds.
Then draw an **X** on **8** birdhouses.

125

The Number 9

Grover is a good waiter. He keeps everyone's water glass full!

  Count and color **9** glasses.

  Trace the number **9**. Then write some of your own.

126

Count to 9

Color **9** saucers.
Then draw more teacups to make **9** in all.

127

The Number 10

Baby Natasha likes the sound of rattles.

 Count and color **10** rattles.

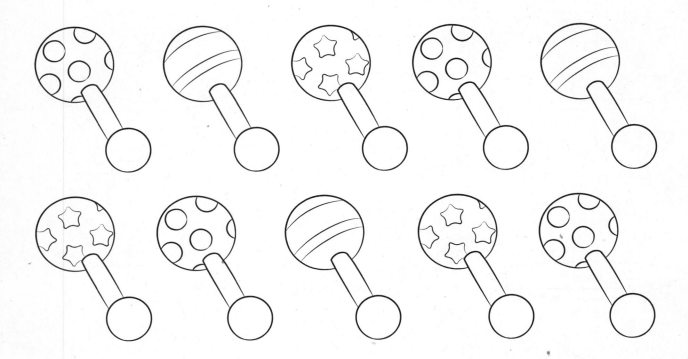

  Trace the number **10**. Then write some of your own.

(128)

Count to 10

 Circle each group with **10**.

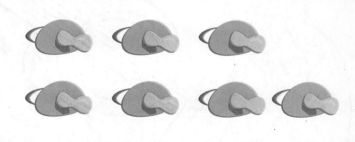

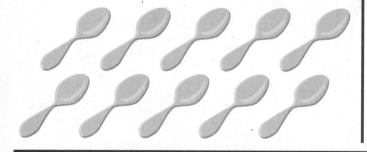

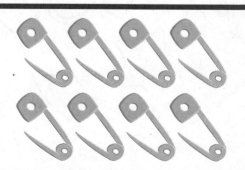

Color by Number

  Say the numbers in the picture.
Then color the spaces using the color key.

6=    7=    8=    9=   10=

Count Your Vegetables

  Look at the number. Count and circle the same number of items for each row.

9

7

10

6

8

131

The Number 11

Baby Bear is coloring a picture.

  Count and color **11** crayons.

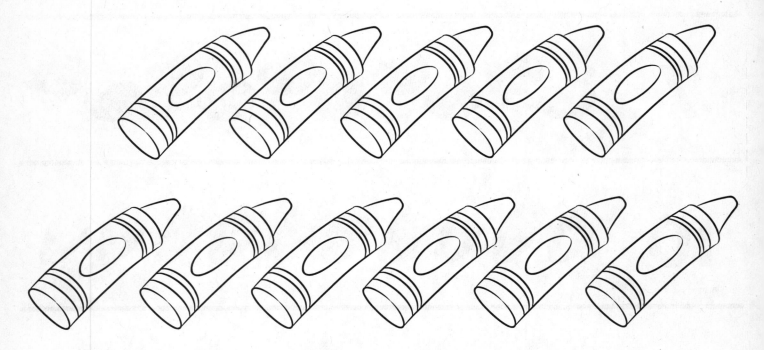

Trace the number **11**. Then write some of your own.

132

  Count the objects in each group.
Then write the number that shows how many.

_____

- - - - - - - - - - -

_____

_____

- - - - - - - - - - -

_____

_____

- - - - - - - - - - -

_____

Explore More ■ ◆ ● ■ ◆ ● ■ ◆ ● ■ ◆ ●

Play a number guessing game with your child. With your finger, write the number
11 on your child's back. See if she can guess the number. Then practice with other
numbers your child has learned.

133

The Number 12

Telly Monster can never have enough triangles.

  Count and color **12** triangles.

  Trace the number **12.** Then write some of your own.

12 12

Count to 12

  Count the donuts.
Then draw more to make 12 in all.

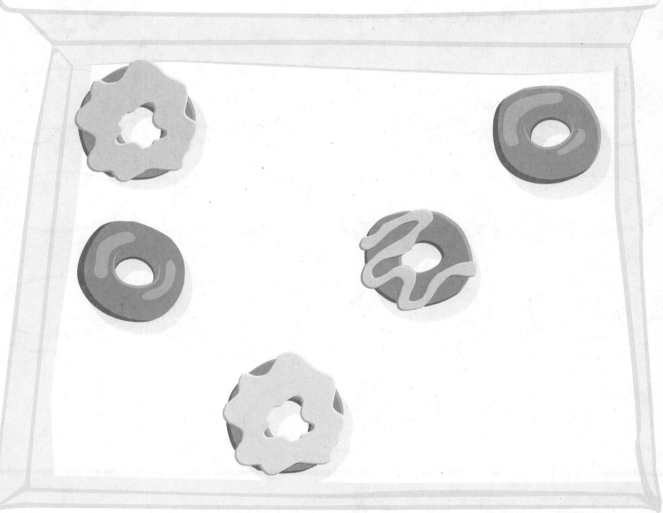

Explore More ■ ◆ ● ■ ● ◆ ● ■ ◆ ●

There are dozens of ways to practice counting! Place objects such as buttons, paper clips, or dry cereal, in an empty egg carton. Have your child use the objects to count to 12.

The Number 13

Bert is proud of his bottle cap collection.

  Count and color **13** bottle caps.

  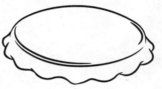 

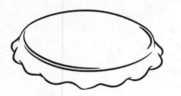   

 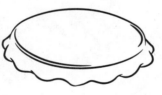  

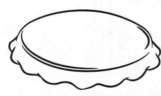

  Trace the number **13**. Then write some of your own.

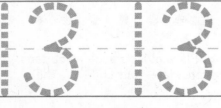

Count to 13

 Draw lines from **13** pennies to the piggy bank.

Explore More ◼ ◆ ● ◼ ◆ ● ◼ ◆ ● ◼ ◆ ● ◼ ◆

A fun way to practice counting is to use a coin collection or whatever type of collection you may have. Help your child lay out the collection in groups of up to **13** items. Then encourage him to count the items in each group.

137

The Number 14

14 fourteen

Ernie and The Count can always count on their friends.

  Count and color **14** Twiddle Bugs.

  Trace the number **14**. Then write some of your own.

14 14

Count to 14

 Circle the group with **14**.

 Draw **14** spots on the bug.

Ready, Set, Preschool! Learn About Counting   **SESAME STREET** 123

The Number 15

15 fifteen

Oscar loves old stinky socks.

  Count and color **15** stinky socks.

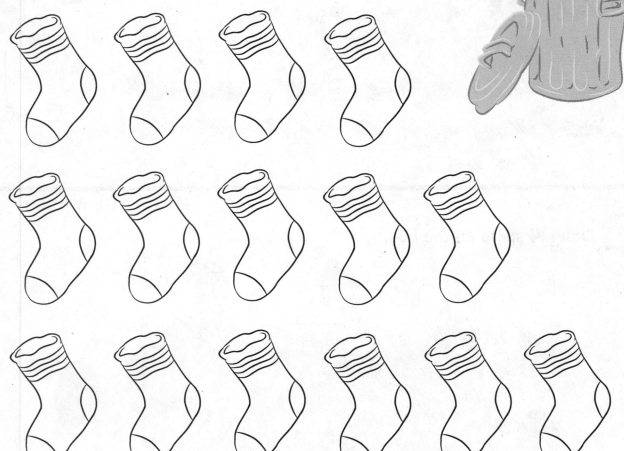

  Trace the number **15**. Then write some of your own.

15 15

Count to 15

 Circle each group with **15**.

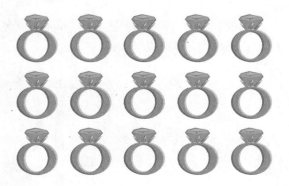

141

Gone Fishing

  Count the fish. Then draw a line from each group to the number that shows how many.

12

15

8

5

11

Ready, Set, Preschool! Learn About Counting

Musical Monster

  Draw lines to connect the dots from 1 to 15. Then color the instrument.

143

The Number 16

Prairie Dawn is watering flowers in the garden.

  Count and color **16** flowers.

 Trace the number **16**. Then write some of your own.

(144)

16 16

Count to 16

Count and draw an **X** on **16** pumpkins.

16

Explore More

Make a sweet **16** collage with your child using old magazines and newspapers. Help your child cut out pictures that show **16** of her favorite things. Talk about each thing and then glue the pictures onto a sheet of paper to make a collage.

Ready, Set, Preschool! Learn About Counting

The Number 17

The Amazing Mumford has made lots of rabbits appear.

  Count and color **17** rabbits.

  Trace the number **17**. Then write some of your own.

146

Count to 17

  Count and circle **17** favorite pets.

147

SESAME STREET

The Number 18

18 eighteen

Elmo is shopping for a new bowl for his friend Dorothy.

 Count and color **18** bowls.

 Trace the number **18**. Then write some of your own.

18 18

148

Count to 18

  Count the fish.
Then draw more to make **18** in all.

149

SESAME STREET

The Number 19

19 nineteen

Zoe has lots of hats to try on.

 Count and color **19** hats.

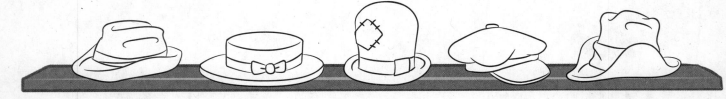

 Trace the number **19**. Then write some of your own.

19 19

Count to 19

19

Count and color **19** circles.

Explore More

Magnetic numbers are a great way to reinforce number recognition. Put a set on your refrigerator door or on a cookie sheet. Say the numbers and have your child point to and repeat each number. You can also choose three numbers and have your child arrange them in numerical order.

151

The Number 20

20 twenty

Big Bird is finding plenty of pretty seashells.

  Count and color **20** shells.

  Trace the number **20**. Then write some of your own.

152

Count to 20

  Count and write the number of dog bones in each group.

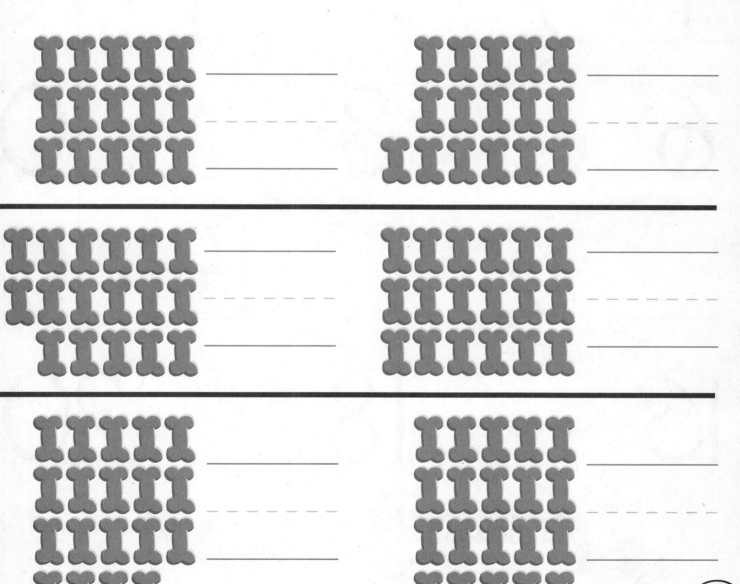

Ready, Set, Preschool! Learn About Counting

SESAME STREET

Keep on Counting!

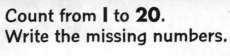 Count from **1** to **20**.
Write the missing numbers.

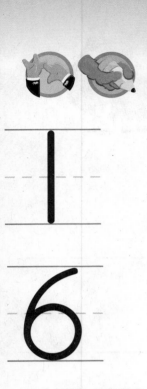

1 2 ___ 4

6 ___ 8 10

___ 12 ___ 14 15

16 ___ 18 ___ 20

 Ready, Set, Preschool! Learn About Counting

Before and After

 Write the number that comes right **before** each number.

——————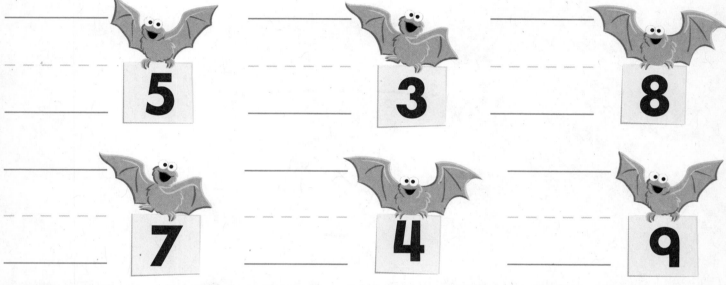
5

——————   **3**

——————   **8**

——————   **7**

——————   **4**

——————   **9**

 Write the number that comes right **after** each number.

1 ——————

6 ——————

3 ——————

5 ——————

2 ——————

7 ——————

Ready, Set, Preschool! Learn About Counting

SESAME STREET

Counting Review

Elmo can count to **20**. Can you?

  Draw a line to follow the numbers from **1** to **20**. Then, color the picture.

1 **20**

2

3 o o o o o o **19**

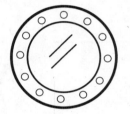

4 **18**

5 **17**

6 **16**

7 **10** **11** **12** **13**

9 **8** **14** **15**

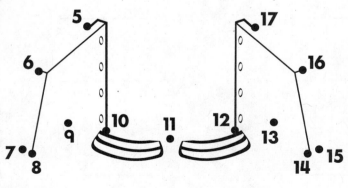

SESAME STREET Ready, Set, Preschool! Learn About Counting

Zoe Can Count

Look closely at the picture. How many do you see?

Count each animal. Then write how many.

_____

_____

_____

_____

157

Counting Party!

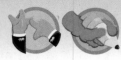

Count the friends at the party.
Then write how many.

How many friends?
_____

- - - - - - - - - - - -

_____

How many balloons?
_____

- - - - - - - - - - - -

_____

Draw and color **10** more balloons to make **20** in all.

Hidden Numbers 1-15

Look closely at the picture below.
Find and circle the hidden numbers **1** to **15**.

Ready, Set, Preschool! Learn About Counting

SESAME STREET

Index